I pledge allegiance to the flag

of the United States of America,

and to the republic

for which it stands,

one nation under God,

indivisible,

with liberty and justice for all.

I Pledge Allegiance

by

Pat Mora & Libby Martinez

illustrated by

Patrice Barton

Alfred A. Knopf
New York

On Monday when I get to school, my teacher, Mrs. Adams, asks, "Did your great-aunt pass her test?"

"Yes!" I say. "She is very smart."

I tell my class all about my great-aunt. She is eighty years old, and my family calls her Lobo, which means "wolf" in Spanish. (She calls *us* her *lobitos*—her "little wolves.")

Lobo studied very hard. She learned all about America.
"That's wonderful!" says Mrs. Adams. "Libby's great-
aunt passed her citizenship test!"
My teacher claps. My class and I clap, too.

On Friday, Mom and I will go with my great-aunt to a
special place. She will say the Pledge of Allegiance, and she
will become a citizen of the United States. She is going to
practice all week so she won't make any mistakes.

"We're going to practice the Pledge of Allegiance this week, too," says Mrs. Adams. "On Thursday, Libby can lead us in saying the Pledge so she will be ready for her great-aunt's special ceremony on Friday. Will you do that, Libby?"

"Yes," I say. I like being in front of the class. I hope I can remember all of the words.

Mrs. Adams says, "Long ago, in 1892, a man named Francis Bellamy wrote the Pledge of Allegiance. He hoped that girls and boys would promise to be good citizens. Now, let's all read the Pledge together."

I pledge allegiance to the flag

of the United States of America,

and to the republic

for which it stands,

one nation under God,

indivisible,

with liberty and justice for all.

My teacher points to one of the words.

"In-di-vis-i-ble," she says. "It's a big word. It means that there are fifty states, but we are all one country."

After school, my teacher gives my great-aunt
a big congratulations hug.

On the way home, I tell Lobo that my class is practicing the Pledge all week. "On Thursday, I will have to say it in front of everyone!" I say. "I'm a little nervous."

"Let's practice together," she says, and squeezes my hand.

At home, Lobo and I help Mom make enchiladas.
Mom says, "Monday, Tuesday, Wednesday, Thursday…
Friday—a special day."

"Ready to practice, Lobo?" I ask after dinner.

Lobo reads the Pledge, and then she and I say it together for Mom and my kitten, Gloria, my *gatita*:

"I pledge allegiance to the flag of the United States of America, and to the republic for which it stands, one nation under God, indivisible, with liberty and justice for all."

Lobo and I practice again on Tuesday night.

"When we say the Pledge at school, we stand very
straight, like a tree," I tell her. "We put our right hand over
our heart. My teacher says the Pledge of Allegiance is very
special. It's a promise you make with your heart."

"I like the words 'liberty and justice for all,'" says Lobo. "We are promising to be fair to everyone. This country is like one big family, *una familia*, that works together to take care of people who need our help. That is what America did for me."

On Wednesday night, Lobo and I say the Pledge in front of my stuffed animals. They are very good students. I like being the teacher. Tomorrow, I will say the Pledge in front of the whole class.

"Time for bed," says Mom.

I ask Lobo to tuck me in and tell me a story, *un cuento*. I like Lobo's stories. "Why do you want to be a citizen?" I ask.

"*Mi querida*, I was born in Mexico and went to school there, but the United States has been my home for many years. I am proud to be from Mexico and to speak Spanish *and* English. Many people are proud of the places where they were born or where they grew up.

"But a long time ago, when I was a young girl, my father wanted a safer place for us to grow up, and we came to the United States. The American flag—red, white, and blue— wrapped itself around me to protect me."

Lobo tucks my blanket around me.

"The flag made me feel like this," she says.

"Safe and warm."

Lobo smiles and kisses my forehead.

"You will do just fine tomorrow," she says.

On Thursday, Mrs. Adams says, "Libby, would you like to lead our class in saying the Pledge?"

I walk to the front of the room. Everyone is looking at me. I think of Lobo's smile. I stand up very straight and put my hand over my heart. I take a deep breath.

Together we say, "I pledge allegiance to the flag of the United States of America, and to the republic for which it stands, one nation under God, indivisible, with liberty and justice for all."

At home, I tell my mom and Lobo that I
remembered all the words. Lobo and I practice
one more time. Mom claps and hugs us.

On Friday, Lobo wears a new blue dress. Mom, Lobo,
and I hold hands when we walk into a big room. There
are so many people! A woman in a black robe stands at the
front of the room. She looks like a judge on TV. We all sit
down. Everyone is very quiet.

The judge says, "Today is a happy day." She asks all the
new citizens to stand.

Mom whispers that I can stand with Lobo. The judge says, "Please place your right hand over your heart."

Lobo and I stand very straight, like trees. We put our hand over our heart. We smile.

Then we both say, "I pledge allegiance to the flag of the United States of America."

Authors' Note

Our aunt Ygnacia Delgado was a very special lady. A young woman during the Mexican Revolution of 1910, she came to El Paso, Texas, with her sisters and father, who had been a circuit judge in northern Mexico. She never married and often lived with our family. When she'd arrive in the evening after work, she'd call out, *"¿Dónde están mis lobitos?"* ("Where are my little wolves?") We all began calling her Lobo and not *tía,* which means "aunt" in Spanish.

Lobo learned English when she arrived in the United States. She liked books and read encyclopedias, newspapers, and prayer books in Spanish and English. Lobo always wore dresses. She was very devout, very proper.

Lobo became a U.S. citizen in her late seventies and did give the wonderful answer about why she became a citizen that we refer to in the book. Although she had studied hard for her citizenship test, the judge only asked her one question. "Miss Delgado, who is the president of the United States?"

Lobo was everything a citizen should be—hardworking, honest, brave, respectful, responsible. And even in her nineties, Lobo was fun. She read to us and played games with us. We all remember her smile.

This book is our first collaboration. It's an honor to share the story of our intelligent and loving aunt.

—Pat Mora and Libby Martinez

The words to the original Pledge, written by Francis Bellamy, were published in *The Youth's Companion,* a popular children's magazine, in 1892. The original Pledge has been modified four times.

Ygnacia is pronounced eeg-NAH-see-ah.

In loving memory of our dear aunt Lobo,
and to all new citizens of the United States
—P.M. & L.M.

For my dear aunt Pam
—P.B.

THIS IS A BORZOI BOOK PUBLISHED BY ALFRED A. KNOPF

Text copyright © 2014 by Pat Mora and Libby Martinez

Jacket art and interior illustrations copyright © 2014 by Patrice Barton

All rights reserved. Published in the United States by Alfred A. Knopf,

an imprint of Random House Children's Books, a division of Random House, Inc., New York.

Knopf, Borzoi Books, and the colophon are registered trademarks of Random House, Inc.

Visit us on the Web! randomhouse.com/kids

Educators and librarians, for a variety of teaching tools, visit us at RHTeachersLibrarians.com

Library of Congress Cataloging-in-Publication Data

Mora, Pat.

I pledge allegiance / by Pat Mora and Libby Martinez ; illustrations by Patrice Barton. — 1st ed.

p. cm.

Summary: "Libby and her great-aunt, Lobo, both learn the Pledge of Allegiance—Libby for school,

and Lobo for her U.S. citizenship ceremony." —Provided by publisher.

ISBN 978-0-307-93181-8 (trade) — ISBN 978-0-375-97109-9 (lib. bdg.) — ISBN 978-0-307-97556-0 (ebook)

[1. Pledge of Allegiance—Fiction. 2. Citizenship—Fiction. 3. Schools—Fiction. 4. Great-aunts—Fiction.

5. Mexican Americans—Fiction.] I. Martinez, Libby. II. Barton, Patrice, illustrator. III. Title.

PZ7.M78819lak 2014   [E]—dc23   2013009711

The illustrations in this book were created using pencil sketches painted digitally.

MANUFACTURED IN CHINA   April 2014   10 9 8 7 6 5 4 3 2 1   First Edition

I pledge allegiance to the flag
of the United States of America,
and to the republic
for which it stands,
one nation under God,
indivisible,
with liberty and justice for all.